PUZZLE CASTLE

Susannah Leigh

Illustrated by Brenda Haw

Designed by Paul Greenleaf

Contents

Series Editor: Gaby Waters

About this story

This story is about a brave knight called Sophie and her adventure at Puzzle Castle. There is a puzzle on every double page. Solve them all and help Sophie on her way. If you get stuck, look at the answers on pages 31 and 32.

This is Sophie, the brave knight. She lives in a village not far from Puzzle Castle.

This is Puzzle Castle.

Sophie's friend, Titus the Timid, lives in Puzzle Castle. He has written Sophie a letter. Here it is.

This is Titus. He is wearing his banquet outfit.

Puzzle Castle
Monday

Dear Sophie,

You are invited to a grand banquet in Puzzle Castle today, but first we need your help. For the past three days there has been a monster in the dungeons. No one has seen it, but everyone is very scared. You are the bravest person I know. Could you come early and get rid of it? I will meet you in the castle courtyard at three o'clock.

Love from your friend, Titus.

P.S. I will be wearing my banquet outfit!

Useful equipment

When Sophie gets to the castle she will need to find ten things that may come in handy when she reaches the dungeons. You will find one object on every double page, from the moment she enters the castle, until she arrives at the monster's lair...

umbrella

powerful flashlight

monster protection shield

run-faster shoes

monster phrase book

key

mystery box

extra-brave toffees

monster protection helmet

useful string

Cecil the castle ghost

Puzzle Castle is haunted by a very friendly ghost. His name is Cecil. He is hiding spookily on every double page. See if you can spot him.

Jester Jim

Jester Jim is practising his juggling for the banquet, but he's not very good at it. He has lost his juggling balls around the castle. There is at least one hiding on every double page. Can you find them?

The juggling balls look like this.

The adventure starts

On the day of the grand banquet, Sophie set out for Puzzle Castle. As she drew near, the castle loomed ahead of her, surrounded by a monstrous moat. Peering down into the water she saw strange creatures and big fish with snappy teeth.

The only way across the water was by the many bridges. But this wasn't as easy as it looked. Some of the bridges were broken and others were too dangerous to cross. Sophie would have to be very careful.

Can you find a safe route across the moat?

Bye!

Where is Titus?

Sophie jumped to the safety of the bank. She bounded up to the castle gate and pulled the bell which jangled loudly. The gate rose slowly and Sophie stepped into the bustling courtyard of Puzzle Castle.

Everyone was busy preparing for the grand banquet and trying hard not to think about the monster in the dungeons. It was nearly three o' clock. Sophie looked out for Titus. She was sure he was hiding somewhere.

Can you see Titus?

I must start looking for my useful equipment.

Sophie's instructions

"Don't worry, Titus, I'll deal with the monster," said Sophie bravely. "Lead me to the dungeons."

"Oh no, Sophie," Titus shivered. "You are brave enough to find the monster by yourself. Here's a plan of Puzzle Castle, and a list of people you will meet on your journey. You must visit each person in turn. Each one needs your help getting ready for the banquet. Help them out and you will soon find your way to the dungeons."

Can you match the people with the rooms where Sophie is most likely to find them?

FIND THESE PEOPLE ON THE WAY

MERVIN, Portrait Keeper

PRINCESS POSY

LARRY, Look-out boy

BETH the Babysitter

MRS. CRUMB the Cook

WIZARD WILF

PLAN OF
PUZZLE CASTLE

Lookout Tower

Round Room

Dressing Room

Posy's Room

Portrait Room

Entrance Hall

Banquet Hall

Jim's Room

Chapel

Babies' Room

The Kitchen

Wilf's Den

Tall Room

The Cellar

Cog Room

Dungeons

9

Royal portraits

Sophie promised to see Titus later and began her journey. Her first stop was the portrait gallery.

"Sophie," cried Mervin the portrait keeper. "Princess Posy's Uncle Edwin is coming all the way from Gruldavia for the banquet. I have to meet him, but I've forgotten what he looks like. If I get this wrong, I'll be thrown in the dungeons. His picture is here. He has black hair, a beard and a moustache. He always wears red and purple. He has no children and he doesn't like horses."

Can you find Uncle Edwin's picture?

Does Uncle Edwin have big ears?

Princess Posy's problem

Sophie curtsied as she entered Princess Posy's room. What a mess it was!

"Sophie!" cried Posy. "I know you're going to fight the monster, but I've got a bigger problem. I want to wear my matching necklace, bracelet, ring and crown to the banquet. I can't find them in my big wooden chest."

Can you find a necklace, a bracelet, a ring and a crown that match?

The look-out tower

Sophie left Posy admiring her jewels, and climbed up to the castle battlements. Here she found Larry the look-out boy, pointing to a lot of people approaching the castle.

"Sophie!" he cried. "All these people are arriving for the grand banquet, but I don't know if they've been invited."

Banquet guest list

BARON BORIS the BAD and his BADDIES (not invited - deserves 3 bad eggs)

SIR HORACE and his HORRIBLES (not invited - deserves soup treatment)

SIR NICE NED and his FRIENDS (invited)

COUNT CURTIS and his CRAFTY COUSINS (not invited - bubbling treacle treatment)

LADY LUCY LOVELY and FRIENDS (invited)

FEARLESS FREDA and FRIENDS (invited)

NASTY KNIGHT KEVIN and NASTIES (not invited - aim rubber arrows at him)

WONDERFUL WANDA and her FRIENDS (invited)

BAD EGGS

DUNG

SOUP

BUBBLING TREACLE

Sophie read the guest list. Then she looked at the flags of the approaching groups and checked to see if they were invited or not.

Do you know who is invited to the banquet?

Beth and the babies

Sophie scrambled down to the babies' room. Here she found Beth, the very new babysitter, and lots of naughty babies.

"Sophie," cried Beth. "I have to dress the babies for the banquet, but I don't know which clothes belong to which baby. I've even forgotten each baby's name!"

Sophie looked at the party outfits hanging on the wall. Then she looked at the babies in their underwear. Soon she had matched them together.

Can you find the right outfit for each baby?

Frank

Whee!

Goo

Ha Ha!

Monster

Puzzle Castle

$2 + 2 =$
$3 + 1 =$
$4 + 1 =$

16

In the kitchen

Sophie left Beth with the smartly dressed babies and followed the smell of burnt banquet buns to the kitchen. The grand banquet feast was boiling away, but Mrs. Crumb the cook was flustered.

"I wanted to make you a monster-fighting pudding to build up your strength, Sophie," she said. "But some rascal has hidden the ingredients. I've lost two red plums, a pot of honey, three fresh eggs, four loaves of bread and a lemon."

Can you find the missing pudding ingredients?

COOKIES

Mustard

biscuits

19

Which way now?

"I'll have to eat that pudding later!" Sophie called, as she dropped through the trapdoor. She climbed down some steep steps. To the right was a door. She pushed it open and walked into a room with cogs hanging from the ceiling. There was no one here, so Sophie decided to move on.

Her next stop was Wizard Wilf's den. But which door led to it? There were six to choose from, but danger lurked behind almost every one. Sophie looked at her castle plan and soon knew which door to take.

Which door should Sophie choose?

The wizard's den

Wizard Wilf's Den
it's secret!

Sophie pushed open the door and walked down a small passageway to another door. Through this door lay Wizard Wilf's secret den. Wilf stood stirring a big pot.

"Sophie," he cried. "I'm brewing a magic potion to cast a spell. It will make you invisible and help you dodge the monster."

Before...

Sophie held her breath as Wilf waved his magic wand. There was a purple flash and a puff of smoke, but when it had cleared they saw the spell hadn't quite worked. Sophie was still there, but lots of other things had vanished.

How many things have disappeared?
Can you spot them all?

After...

Witch Hazel

bananas

My pets

101 BEST SPELLS

MAGIC POWDER

useful bones

Sophie finds the way

There was no time to waste. Sophie climbed down Wilf's ladder and crept along an underground passageway. She soon found herself at the beginning of a maze of tunnels. In the distance she could hear the terrible roars of the monster. She didn't want to get lost underground as she made her way towards the roars, so she unravelled her ball of useful string as she went.

Can you find the way to the monster's roars?

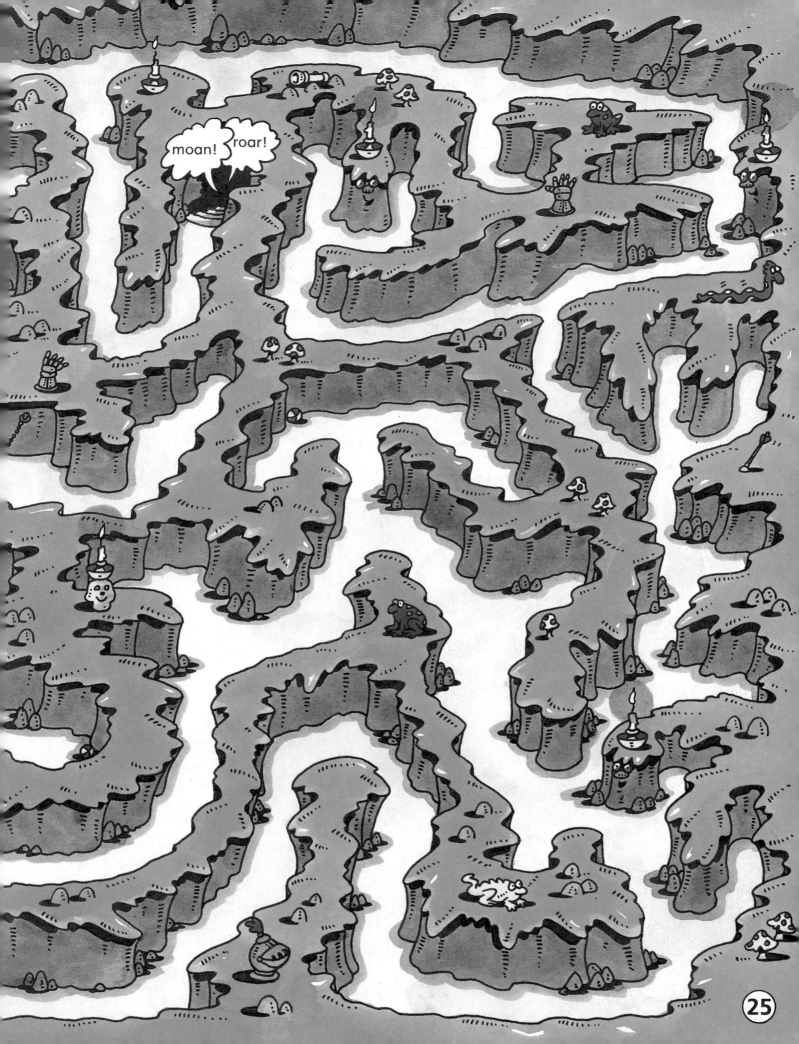

25

The monster's lair...

The rumbling and roaring noise grew louder as Sophie reached the end of the maze. She was at the top of a small flight of steps.

Sophie checked she had all her equipment with her. Chewing nervously on an extra-brave toffee, Sophie began her final journey, down the winding staircase to the monster's lair...

The grand banquet

Dennis cheered up at once. Then Sophie had another idea. She would take him to the banquet. Sophie led Dennis back through the castle and up to the grand banquet hall.

At first everyone was scared of Dennis. But they soon saw he wasn't a monster at all. He was a very friendly little dragon who liked to dance. Everyone was very pleased to see him.

There is someone in this picture who is especially happy to see Dennis. Do you know who it is?

Boris's army pounded past. The ground shook.

Heavy earth fell in front of the tunnel. I was trapped inside.

I saw a tunnel in the hill and I hid inside.

Bedtime story

After the banquet, everyone was very tired. Just before bedtime, Sophie, Titus and Posy curled up with their cups of castle cocoa and listened as Dennis told the story of his adventure at Puzzle Castle . . .

I could only go on, deeper into the tunnel, until I reached the castle dungeon.

Suddenly I saw Boris the Bad and his baddies coming my way. I was very scared.

I was there for three days, getting hungrier and hungrier, until Sophie rescued me.

On Saturday I was playing on the hill beside Puzzle Castle.

I'll never forget the friends I made today.

Answers

Pages 4-5 The adventure starts
The route to the castle is shown in red.

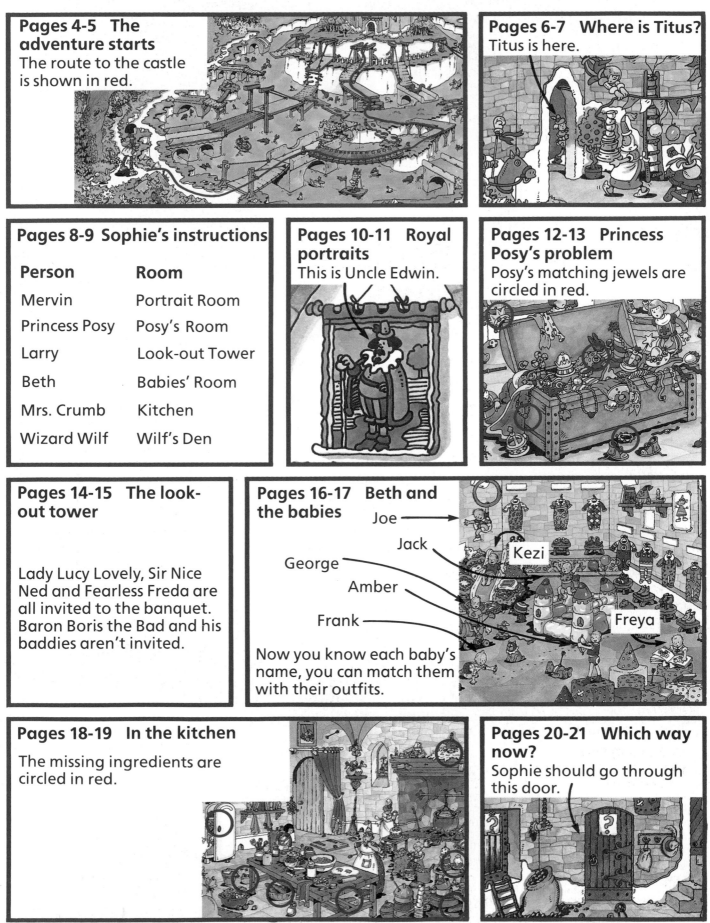

Pages 6-7 Where is Titus?
Titus is here.

Pages 8-9 Sophie's instructions

Person	Room
Mervin	Portrait Room
Princess Posy	Posy's Room
Larry	Look-out Tower
Beth	Babies' Room
Mrs. Crumb	Kitchen
Wizard Wilf	Wilf's Den

Pages 10-11 Royal portraits
This is Uncle Edwin.

Pages 12-13 Princess Posy's problem
Posy's matching jewels are circled in red.

Pages 14-15 The look-out tower
Lady Lucy Lovely, Sir Nice Ned and Fearless Freda are all invited to the banquet. Baron Boris the Bad and his baddies aren't invited.

Pages 16-17 Beth and the babies
Joe
Jack
Kezi
George
Amber
Freya
Frank

Now you know each baby's name, you can match them with their outfits.

Pages 18-19 In the kitchen
The missing ingredients are circled in red.

Pages 20-21 Which way now?
Sophie should go through this door.

Pages 22-23
The wizard's den
The red circles show where Wilf's things were.

Pages 24-25
Sophie finds the way
The way to the monster is shown in red.

Pages 26-27   The monster's lair...
Sophie gives Dennis the mystery box she found in the wizard's den. It is a dragon-in-a-box!

Pages 28-29   The grand banquet
Dennis's mum is especially happy to see him. Here she is.

Did you spot everything?

Juggling balls	Useful equipment	Cecil the ghost

The chart below shows you how many juggling balls are hidden on each double page. You can also find out which piece of Sophie's useful equipment is hidden where.

Did you remember to look out for Cecil the ghost? He is hiding spookily on every double page. Look back through the book again and see if you can find him.

Pages	Juggling balls	Useful equipment
4-5	one	none here!
6-7	four	monster protection shield
8-9	one	key
10-11	three	useful string
12-13	four	run-faster shoes
14-15	two	umbrella
16-17	three	monster phrase book
18-19	five	extra-brave toffees
20-21	two	monster protection helmet
22-23	three (or is it six?)	mystery box
24-25	four	powerful flashlight
26-27	one	none here!
28-29	nineteen	none here!

Four friends

Now Sophie, Titus, Dennis and Princess Posy are very good friends. Every Saturday when the sun is shining, they play on the hill beside Puzzle Castle. If it's raining, they eat toast and cakes in Posy's room, and Jester Jim teaches them how to juggle. And because he has three new friends to play with, Dennis isn't afraid of Boris the Bad anymore.

PUZZLE PLANET

Susannah Leigh

Illustrated by Brenda Haw

Designed by Paul Greenleaf

Contents

Series Editor: Gaby Waters

About this story

This story is about a young astronaut called Archie, his robot Blip, and their adventures on Puzzle Planet. There is a puzzle on every double page. See if you can solve them all. If you get stuck, you can look at the answers on pages 63 and 64.

Space school report

NAME: Archie

SUBJECT	GRADE
STAR SPOTTING	A+
ROCKET FLYING	A+
MOON WALKING	A+

Comment: Archie is a very helpful member of class.

Archie

Blip

Archie's space base

Archie's school report

Archie is a junior astronaut who goes to space school. One day, in the summer, he gets a surprise letter. It is from the wisest astronaut teacher of them all, Professor Moon. Here is the letter.

Puzzle Planet

Professor Moon

Golden Palace
Puzzle Planet
Wednesday

To: Archie
Space base
Planet Earthy Minor

Dear Archie,

I have read your space school report. Well done! Now you and some of your school friends have the chance to prove your skills as astronauts. You must travel to Puzzle Planet and find me in my Golden Palace by 4 o'clock on Thursday. If you succeed, I will award you with a special space badge which I only give to the bravest young astronauts in the universe.

From Professor Moon.

P.S. I will send you a kit list of the things you need to bring to Puzzle Planet

Things to spot

All good astronauts are observant. As soon as Archie arrives on Puzzle Planet, he must prove he is a good astronaut by spotting some special objects. These objects can only be found on Puzzle Planet. There is one hiding on each double page, from the moment Archie lands. Here they are.

giant pink marshmallow

bread fruit tree

Puzzle Planet bug

Puzzle Planet flag

red rock

friendly toffee apple

Puzzle Planet pencil

scaley goldfish

green spider

star plant

footprint

Sneaky Sydney
Sydney lives on Puzzle Planet. He's a bit of a bully and likes spoiling people's games. Look out for Sydney's spy satellite. It's watching Archie on every double page.

Sydney's spy satellite.

Sydney

Space newts
Puzzle Planet is the home of the pink space newts. There is at least one newt hiding on every double page, from the time Archie lands on Puzzle Planet. Look out for them!

Now turn the page to begin the adventure!

Getting ready

Archie was looking forward to his very first visit to Puzzle Planet. Outside, his rocket was parked and was nearly ready for take off.

Archie looked at the kit list Professor Moon had sent him. It showed six useful things he would need to take to Puzzle Planet. Archie looked around his small space base in dismay. It was such a mess, how would he ever find the six things on the list?

Can you find the six things Archie needs?

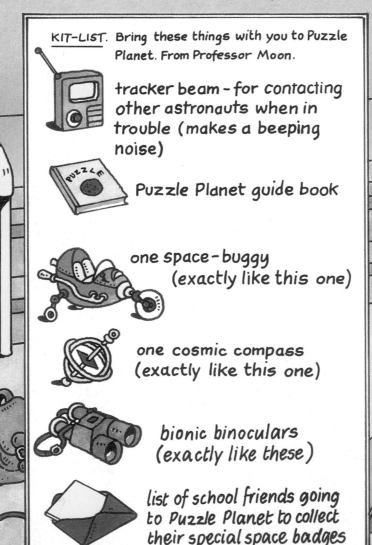

KIT-LIST. Bring these things with you to Puzzle Planet. From Professor Moon.

tracker beam – for contacting other astronauts when in trouble (makes a beeping noise)

Puzzle Planet guide book

one space-buggy (exactly like this one)

one cosmic compass (exactly like this one)

bionic binoculars (exactly like these)

list of school friends going to Puzzle Planet to collect their special space badges

Star maze

Soon everything was ready for the journey. Now Archie had to plan his route to Puzzle Planet. He peered through his super-powerful telescope. Far, far away, he could see the red glow of Puzzle Planet.

In his little space base, Archie shivered and wondered if he would ever find a path through the twisty maze of stars shining in the galaxy.

Can you help Archie find a way through the star maze to Puzzle Planet?

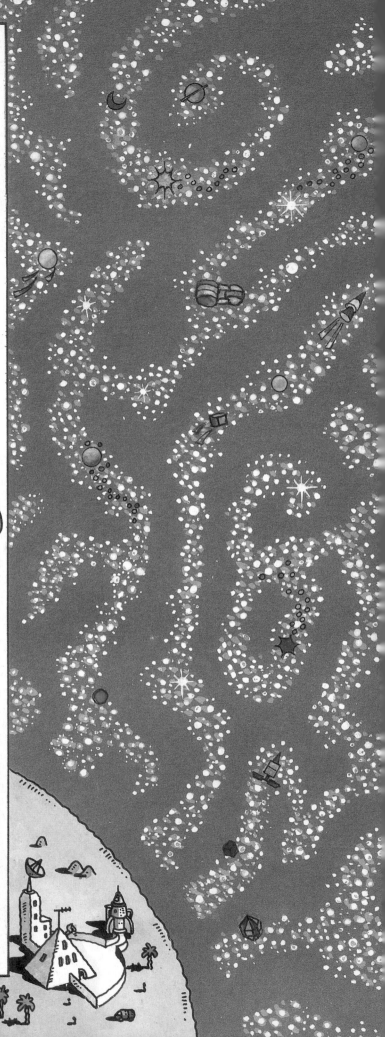

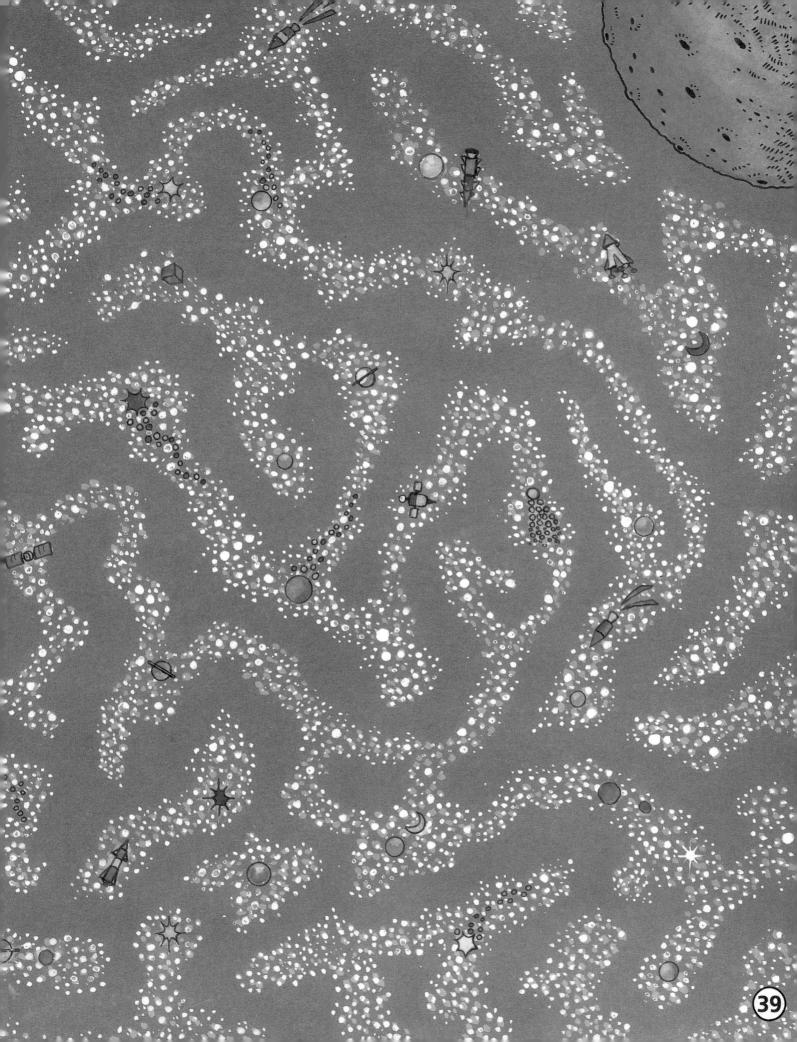

Space journey

At last it was time to set off. Archie made some final flight checks, took his travel-sickness pill and called to Blip. The two friends climbed aboard the space rocket. They closed the outer doors, fastened their seat belts and set the controls for Puzzle Planet.

Archie began the countdown. "5...4...3...2...1..."

Planet puzzle

Archie was very pleased to see Blip again. Now they had to find out exactly where they were on Puzzle Planet.

Archie spun his cosmic compass and walked a little way north into a small clearing. There were lots of strange things to look at. Archie got out his Puzzle Planet guide book and turned to the page he needed. He looked at the pictures carefully. By matching the pictures with what he saw in front of him, he could find out where they were.

Where are they?

WHERE ARE YOU? A scenic guide to Puzzle Planet

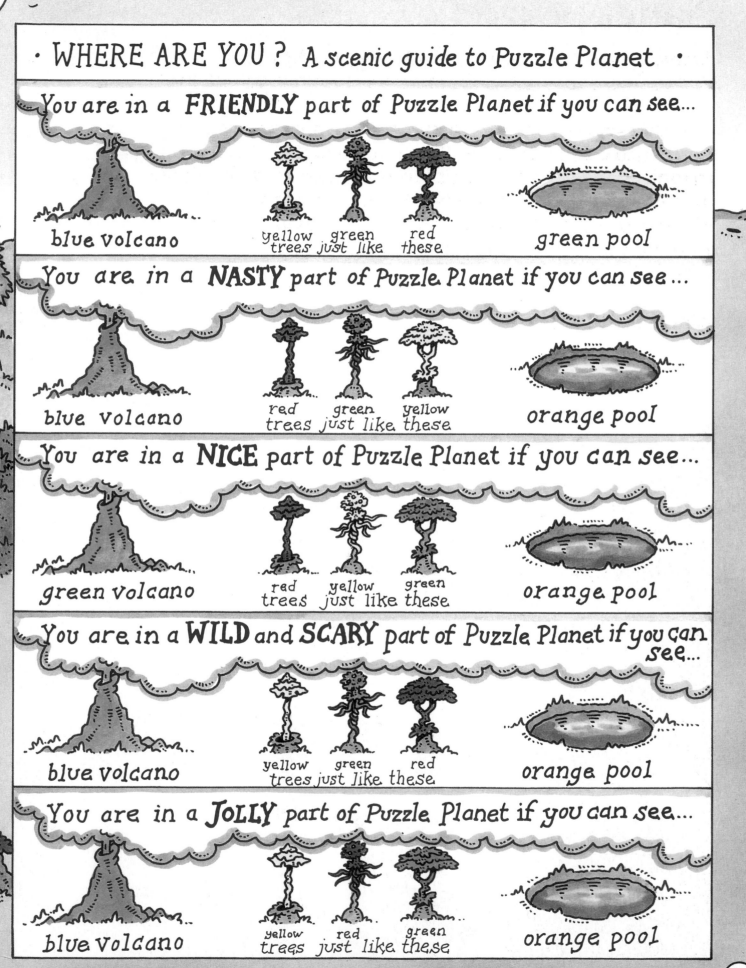

You are in a **FRIENDLY** part of Puzzle Planet if you can see...

blue volcano — yellow trees — green just like — red these — green pool

You are in a **NASTY** part of Puzzle Planet if you can see...

blue volcano — red trees — green just like — yellow these — orange pool

You are in a **NICE** part of Puzzle Planet if you can see...

green volcano — red trees — yellow just like — green these — orange pool

You are in a **WILD** and **SCARY** part of Puzzle Planet if you can see...

blue volcano — yellow trees just like — green these — red — orange pool

You are in a **JOLLY** part of Puzzle Planet if you can see...

blue volcano — yellow trees — red just like — green these — orange pool

Archie in trouble

Archie gulped. They were in a wild and scary part of Puzzle Planet! Suddenly there was a buzzing noise behind them. Archie spun around. It came from the rocket wreck. Archie and Blip rushed over to investigate. The video screen was on and someone was sending a message. It was Sydney, the space school bully.

"Archie, my magnetic field made you crash. I have done the same to three of your two-eyed, two-eared space mates. You won't get your special badges from Professor Moon now. Tee hee."

The picture faded. Archie picked up the list of his school friends who were also on their way to Professor Moon's palace. Archie thought back to Sydney's words, and soon knew which three friends were in trouble, somewhere on Puzzle Planet.

Which of Archie's space friends are in trouble?

Jane from Jupiter

Martin the Martian

Bob from Beta Milennia

Cosmic Ray

Nellie from Neptune

Asteroid Annie

Betty from Blarg

Ollie from Outer Space

Astro Phil

Spacey Sall

Sadie from Saturn

Victor the Vargon

Galactic Greg

Supernova Sam

Pluto Poppy

Milky-way Mary

Pete from Planet Putty

Archie from Earthy Minor

Ice storm

There was no time to lose. Archie had to find his friends. He switched on his tracker beam. If another astronaut was in trouble he'd soon find out. Sure enough, it began to beep. Archie pulled the space-buggy from the wreckage, put it into mega-drive, and zoomed off.

Within seconds they were speeding past strange snowy scenery. Suddenly a huge ball of ice fell from the sky.

"It's an ice-meteor storm!" Archie cried. "We must find shelter before it smashes us into pieces!"

Can you see a safe, empty cave where Archie, Blip and the buggy can find shelter?

Bubble trouble

The storm passed and they drove safely on. Ahead, on top of a small mountain, a rocket had crashed. Someone was in trouble! All of a sudden a big bubble floated past. Trapped inside was Pete from Planet Putty. Archie was about to burst the bubble when he saw another one, with another Pete inside, then another, and another.

"I bet this is Sydney's trick," thought Archie. "Only one is the real Pete. The rest are slightly different."

Which is the real Pete?

You have seen a picture of Pete on page 45.

Spacey swamp

Pete jumped aboard the buggy and they bounced on. Soon they came to a stop at a slimy green swamp. In the middle was Betty from Blarg, trapped on top of her sinking rocket. They had to rescue her and reach the other side to continue their journey.

Pete was an expert on swamps. He knew that there was only one safe way to cross. They must step from one plant or creeper to the next. But they mustn't tread on anything with red spots. They would have to be very careful.

Can you rescue Betty and reach the other side?

Giant snails

Back on dry land, the friends saw a space ship surrounded by giant snails. Inside was a worried Victor the Vargon.

"These slimy creatures are hungry!" he cried.

"It's OK, Victor," yelled Betty. "The Puzzle Planet snails like eating blue space bananas best, and I can see seven, one for each of them!"

Can you find seven blue bananas?

Don't worry!

Following the signal

"Now let's find Professor Moon," said Archie, as the snails began to eat the blue bananas.

They were just wondering which way to go when Archie's tracker beam began to beep. Someone else was in trouble. The noise came from the end of the path ahead.

They ran up the path to a funny shaped building.

The door was open, so they walked slowly inside . . .

The beep got louder.

They followed the noise along a winding passage.

54

At the end was a small room, but there was no one in trouble here. Then Archie knew they had been tricked. There were things in this room he had seen before.

What things has Archie seen before?
Who do you think they belong to?

Trapped!

They were in Sydney's secret hide-out. In the room ahead stood Sydney himself.

"You walked straight into my trap," he smiled. "There's no escape. You won't find Professor Moon now."

Everyone was very scared, but Blip wasn't afraid. He looked at Sydney and his antenna began to twitch. He knew exactly how to make Sydney disappear and give the space friends time to escape.

What can the friends do to make Sydney disappear?

SYDNEY'S BEST TRICKS TO PLAY ON FRIENDS

BLACK HOLE – friend sits in dark for ten mega-minutes

GARBAGE CHUTE – covers friend in galactic garbage

TRAP NET – friend caught inside for six mega-minutes

TELEPORTER – sends friend to an unknown destination for one mega-hour

Canyon maze

Blip flicked the teleporter switch on and Sydney vanished. The friends dived through the door on the other side of the room, pausing to grab some useful skateboards. They skated down a chute and skidded to a stop at the edge of a maze of canyons. In the distance they could see three gold buildings.

"One of those is Professor Moon's palace!" cried Betty. "I recognize it from his letter. We'll skate there in no time."

Which is Professor Moon's palace?
Can you find a way to it?

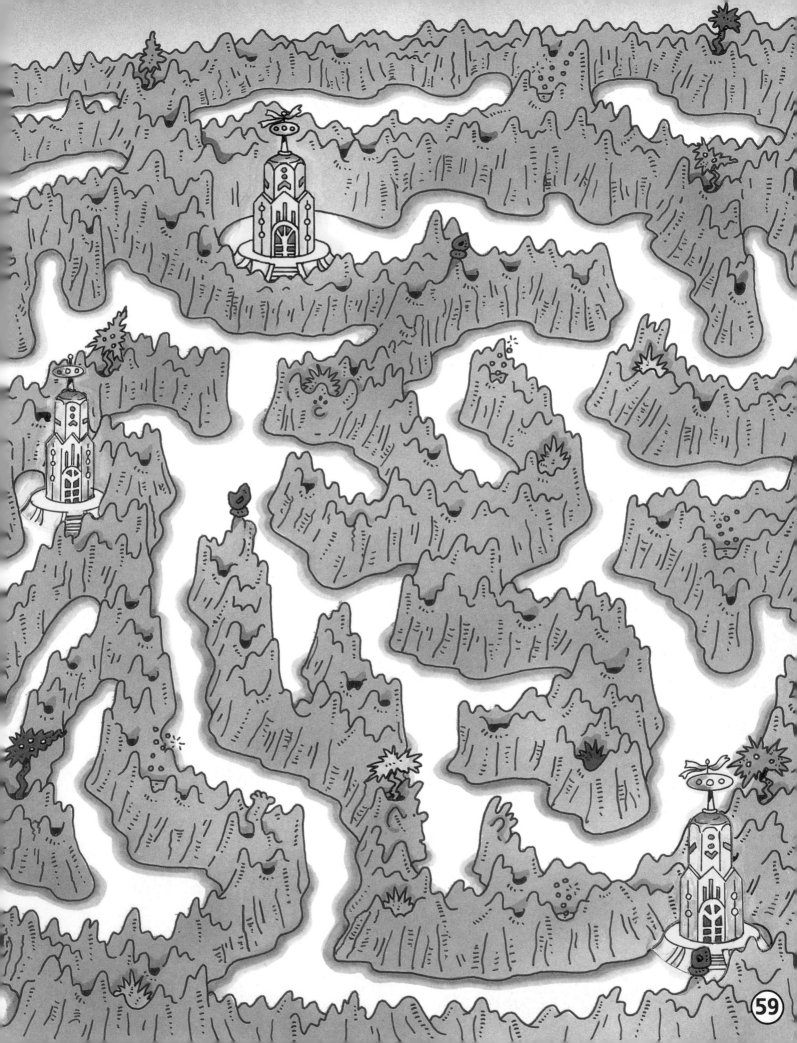

Just in time

Archie and his friends skated into the palace, just as the clock struck four. They saw lots of familiar faces, all smiling and cheering.

"If it wasn't for Archie, we wouldn't have made it to the palace at all," said Betty.

She told everyone about their adventures. Professor Moon gave Archie an extra award for being especially brave. Even Blip had a tasty treat. They were very proud and pleased.

Do you recognize everyone here?
Can you spot the unexpected guest?

Spacey Shortbread

Voldano cake

Planet Pudding

Puzzle Pop

Puzzle Planet creatures

Did you notice that there are some very strange creatures living on Puzzle Planet? Below is a page from Archie's guide book. It shows pictures of some of them.

You can also read about each creature. Whereabouts on Puzzle Planet do you think each one lives? Why not see if you can find them all?

YOU MIGHT SEE...

Angry Armadillo
This hard-shelled creature will nip an astronaut's ankle.

Yellow Billed Bird
Likes to dribble swamp water onto strangers.

Cave Dog
Lives in dark places and enjoys chewing robots.

Galactic Geek
Likes to sharpen its teeth on space buggies.

Ice Bird
Its feathers are as cold as snow. It has an icicle tail.

Plunger Nose
Harmless, unless it sniffs you, and then – watch out!

Beardy Bird
This friendly bird likes having splashy mud baths.

Mushroom Bird
If you touch the red spotted ones, you'll get an itchy rash.

Swamp Serpent
One will suck your socks, the other will chew your toes.

Answers

Pages 36-37 Getting ready
The six things Archie must take to Puzzle Planet are circled in red.

Pages 38-39 Star maze
The way through the star maze to Puzzle Planet is shown in red.

Pages 40-41 Space journey
Blip is here.

Pages 42-43 Planet puzzle
Archie has landed in a wild and scary part of Puzzle Planet.

Pages 44-45 Archie in trouble
The three friends in trouble are:

Betty from Blarg

Victor the Vargon

Pete from Planet Putty

Pages 46-47 Ice storm
Archie, Blip and the buggy can take shelter in this safe and empty cave.

Pages 48-49 Bubble trouble
This is the real Pete.

Pages 50-51 Spacey swamp
The route to Betty, and then to the other side of the swamp is shown in red.

Pages 52-53 Giant snails
The seven blue bananas are circled in red.

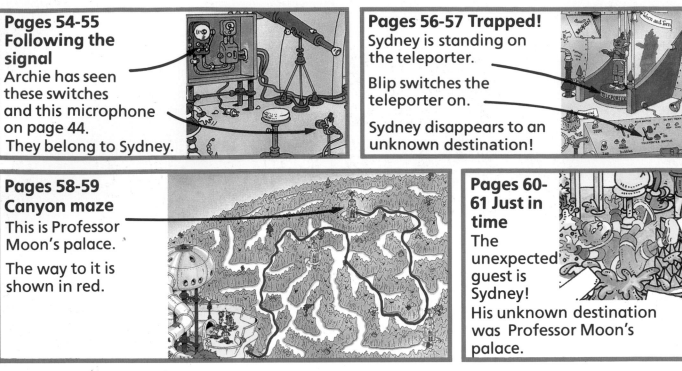

Pages 54-55 Following the signal
Archie has seen these switches and this microphone on page 44. They belong to Sydney.

Pages 56-57 Trapped!
Sydney is standing on the teleporter.

Blip switches the teleporter on.

Sydney disappears to an unknown destination!

Pages 58-59 Canyon maze
This is Professor Moon's palace.

The way to it is shown in red.

Pages 60-61 Just in time
The unexpected guest is Sydney!
His unknown destination was Professor Moon's palace.

Did you spot everything?

Space newts

Things to spot

Spy satellite

Remember that Archie must spot certain things once he arrives on Puzzle Planet. The chart below shows you how many space newts are hiding on each double page. You can also find out which of the Puzzle Planet objects is hidden where.

Did you remember to watch out for Sydney's spy satellite? Look back through the story and see if you can spot the satellite on each double page.

Pages	Space newts	Things to spot
40-41	three	star plant
42-43	three	bread fruit tree
44-45	two	green spider
46-47	one	footprint
48-49	five	Puzzle Planet flag
50-51	three	scaley goldfish
52-53	three	giant pink marshmallow
54-55	three	Puzzle Planet pencil
56-57	one	Puzzle Planet bug
58-59	one	red rock
60-61	five	friendly toffee apple

Something to think about
Although Sydney played some rather sneaky tricks on Archie and his friends, he did make it to Professor Moon's palace in the end. In fact, he was very well-behaved, and only had three helpings of Puzzle pop. Maybe next year it will be Sydney's turn to get his special badge, and be a real astronaut as well. What do you think?

PUZZLE MOUNTAIN

Susannah Leigh

Designed and illustrated by Brenda Haw

Contents

Series Editor: Gaby Waters

About this story

This story is about a brave mountain climber called Poppy Pickaxe, her pet puppy, Bernard, and their adventures on Puzzle Mountain. You will find a puzzle on every double page. See if you can solve them all. If you get stuck, you can look at the answers on pages 95 and 96.

Poppy Pickaxe

Bernard

The people of Puzzle Mountain are having a sports day. Poppy is especially excited because today she will try to climb to the very top of Puzzle Mountain.
Read this poster to find out more.

Puzzle Mountain

CALLING ALL BRAVE MOUNTAIN CLIMBERS!

Can you climb to the very top of Puzzle Mountain?
There is a prize for the first person to get there.

Mountain legend has it that the rare Yodel flower grows on top of Puzzle Mountain.
Take a photo of the flower to prove you've reached the top - but don't pick it!

Yodel flower (artist's impression)

No one has ever reached the very top of Puzzle Mountain before. The way up is difficult and sometimes dangerous. Will Poppy be the first to make it?

Everyone entering the climbing competition must wear a hat with a red ribbon.

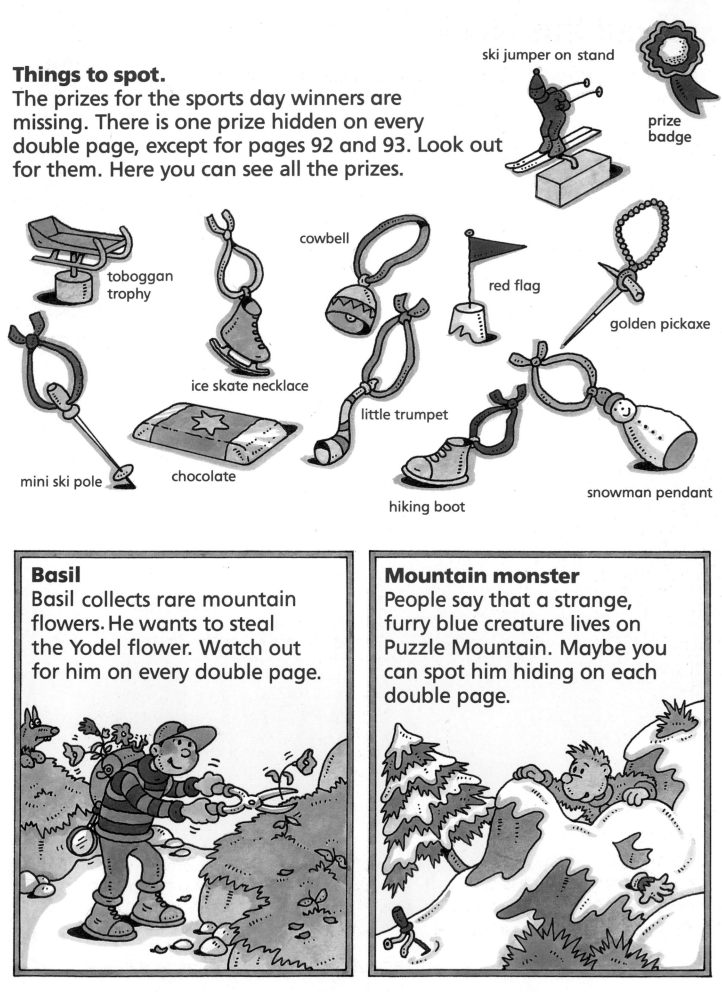

Things to spot.
The prizes for the sports day winners are missing. There is one prize hidden on every double page, except for pages 92 and 93. Look out for them. Here you can see all the prizes.

ski jumper on stand

prize badge

toboggan trophy

cowbell

red flag

golden pickaxe

ice skate necklace

little trumpet

mini ski pole

chocolate

hiking boot

snowman pendant

Basil
Basil collects rare mountain flowers. He wants to steal the Yodel flower. Watch out for him on every double page.

Mountain monster
People say that a strange, furry blue creature lives on Puzzle Mountain. Maybe you can spot him hiding on each double page.

67

Setting off

On the morning of her mountain climb, Poppy stepped out into the bustling village. High above her, far, far in the distance, loomed Puzzle Mountain.

Poppy wondered if the other climbers were as nervous as she was. Then she realized she didn't even know who they were. She remembered that everyone entering the climbing competition had to wear a red ribbon in their hat. Poppy looked around at all the people in the village. She soon spotted the other climbers.

**There are eight other climbers.
Can you spot them?**

SKI SCHOOL

SKI GEAR

HOORAY FOR POPPY!

GOOD LUCK POPPY AND BERNARD

YUM

BUNS

I wonder if Basil's around?

SALE

BARGAIN BIN

Which path?

Poppy took one last look at the village. Then she called to Bernard, and the two friends bravely set off on their expedition.

Before long they arrived at six paths, all leading off in different directions. Only one path led right to the very peak of Puzzle Mountain. Poppy read the information board carefully. Then she looked at the signposts at the beginning of each path. She soon knew which one to take. She could even help the other hikers find their way.

Which path leads to the peak of Puzzle Mountain? Can you find the paths the others want?

Follow the signposts for:

HIKER'S HIGHWAY -

MOUNT LOFTY'S LANE -

WOODLAND WALK -

PUZZLE MOUNTAIN PEAK -

TRICKY TREK -

NUTTY NATURE TRAIL -

I'm looking for the Woodland Walk.

Which way to the Nutty Nature Trail?

HUT

Mountain musicians

Poppy bounded up the path. Soon she heard spluttering noises, and saw an old man trying to conduct a small band of musicians.

"Poppy!" he cried, turning around to face her. "These are the Puzzle Mountain musicians. They are trying to play their instruments, but they are making some very strange sounds."

Suddenly, as the old man spoke, the sound of music started behind him. He spun around. The musicians were now playing their instruments perfectly! The old man turned to Poppy again. He was mystified. What had happened? Poppy looked at the musicians and saw six simple changes that had made all the difference.

Can you spot the differences?

Lost goats

Poppy waved goodbye to the old man and his band and climbed on, further up the mountain path. After a while, she met her friend Gretel the goatherd. Gretel was crying.

"Oh Poppy," she wailed. "The music from those mountain musicians has frightened my goats away. I've lost all seven of them. Can you see them? They are all brown with white faces."

Can you find Gretel's seven lost goats?

ZZZZZZ

Boo hoo!

Ice skating

Leaving the sound of bleating goats behind her, Poppy scrambled along the mountain path. The route was getting steeper, and the air was colder. The path passed by the Puzzle Mountain ice rink, where the skating competition was about to start. The ice was full of people, but four of the contestants looked very glum.

TICKETS

ICE SKATING COMPETITION TODAY

The girls' partners are boys, and the boys' partners are girls.

"Can you help us, Poppy?" they called. "Our skating partners are on the ice somewhere, but we can't find them with all these other people here. Our partners' outfits match our own."

Can you find the four missing skaters?

Food stop

Poppy left the ice skaters and began climbing again, up towards the top of Puzzle Mountain. Soon she came to a small restaurant.

"We've helped a lot of people, Bernard," she said. "It's time we had a treat. Let's get something nice to eat."

Bernard woofed in agreement, and the two friends went inside. There were so many delicious things for sale, they didn't know what to choose. They both wanted something to eat, and to drink, but they only had ten Puzzle Pennies to spend between them.

What can Poppy buy to eat and drink, and what can she buy for Bernard to eat and drink, with just ten Puzzle Pennies?

YUMMY CAKE — 8PP A SLICE

FRUIT — 4PP EACH

EGGS — 4PP EACH

CAKE — 5PP A SLICE

JUICE 3PP A GLASS

CAKE — 6PP A SLICE

DELUXE DRINK — 7PP A GLASS

PASTRIES 2PP EACH

TASTY ROLLS — 3PP EACH

SOUP — 6PP A BOWL

PEOPLE FOOD

PET FOOD

TASTY BONES
2PP EACH

PUPPY FIZZ
7PP A CAN

SAUSAGES
8PP EACH

PUPPY'S
PUDDING—
5PP A SLICE

CHOC DROP
CAKE
7PP A SLICE

DOGGY DRINK
3PP A BOWL

DRINK

BEEFY
BISCUITS
4PP EACH

Slurp.

Yum,
yum.

Ski lift

Poppy licked the crumbs from her lips, and left the restaurant. She set off up the path once more, but stopped when she saw a group of eight grumpy looking skiers.

"We've got to take this ski lift to the other side of the mountain," grumbled the smallest skier. "But this notice has really confused us. Which chairs should each one of us use?"

"Everyone needs help today," thought Poppy as she read the big notice board.

Do you know which skier should use which chair?

Please read instructions before taking lift:

BLUE CHAIR - two adults only

RED CHAIR - one very tall person only

GREEN CHAIR - two adults with hats only

YELLOW CHAIR - cannot hold much weight

PURPLE CHAIR - two children only

RESTAURANT

We always travel together.

Sorting the skis

Poppy couldn't take the ski lift. She had to continue on the mountain path. She puffed and panted her way up. Before long, she bumped into her friend Tim, who was looking at a line of skis stuck into the snow.

"I am in the skiing competition today," he said. "But I can't find my speedy racing skis. I know they are the only matching pair here."

Can you find Tim's matching skis?

I can see two ski poles that match each other.

SKIING COMPETITION HERE

Toboggan race

Dodging the skiers, Poppy pressed on. A little higher up the mountain, she came across a toboggan race that was just about to start. The team that finished the course in the fastest time would be the winner. The three toboggan teams thought the course was very easy, but Poppy wasn't so sure.

"Be careful," she warned. "There are plenty of obstacles and dead ends along the way. Look out for them."

Can you find the clear route from the start to the finish of the race?

Ice walk

Poppy waved goodbye to the toboggan teams and carried on, climbing higher and higher up Puzzle Mountain. Soon there were no more people around, the mist was coming down, and Poppy and Bernard were on their own. They slid across the slippery ground. As they turned a corner, they stopped and gasped.

In front of them was the strangest glacier Poppy had ever seen. Beyond it, towered the very top of Puzzle Mountain. They were nearly there! But first they had to cross the ice, avoiding the deep pools and broken planks. There were two large notices on the glacier. Poppy peered at them through her blizzard-proof binoculars.

To get safely across the glacier, feed the wild snow bears with the six ice cream cones you'll find on the way.

Watch out for WOLVES. They don't eat ice cream.

She couldn't quite believe what she read. Wild snow bears and wolves? She hadn't expected this at all. It was going to be a dangerous journey...

Can you find the safe route across the glacier, picking up the six ice cream cones as you go?

Nearly there

Poppy skidded and slithered across the last of the ice. She landed with a crunch on the snowy bank on the other side of the glacier. Looking up ahead, she could see the peak of Puzzle Mountain, poking through the cloudy mist.

"Follow me, Bernard," she said. And the two friends began the final climb, upward and onward.

The way up was steep and very dangerous.

They hid from huge snowballs.

The air got thinner, and it was difficult to breathe. But at last the mist began to clear...

Poppy was amazed to see spikes of ice rising out of the mountain. Even more surprising were the holes, almost like windows, carved into the icy spikes. Then she spotted something she had only seen a picture of before. She had reached the very top of Puzzle Mountain.

What has Poppy spotted?

Mountain monsters

Click! Poppy took a photo of the Yodel flower. All at once, a huge hairy hand grabbed her arm and pulled her backwards. Poppy blinked, and in a flash she realized she was standing inside a room in a strange ice house. Three blue creatures were looking at her. Poppy rubbed her eyes. She was staring at a family of Puzzle Mountain monsters! Just then, a smaller monster rushed into the room and began to speak.

"I'm sorry I scared you Poppy," said the biggest monster. "But I am the guardian of the Yodel flower and I must protect it. It is the only one in the world, you know. Now I expect you want to get back to the sports day celebrations. Take my super-speedy red toboggan. It will get you down the mountain in no time — if I can find it."

Where is the super-speedy red toboggan?

Poppy returns

Night was falling as Poppy clambered on board the super-speedy red toboggan. She waved goodbye to her new friends, and with a whoosh she and Bernard were off, whizzing down the other side of Puzzle Mountain. As they sped on, Poppy caught a glimpse of Basil, looking very scared. Perhaps now he would think twice before stealing any more mountain flowers.

Can you spot Basil?
Who is scaring him?

Did you spot?

Poppy reached the top of Puzzle Mountain first, and won a golden pickaxe! But whatever happened to the other eight competitors? How far did they get?

Below, you can see pictures of the other climbers, and read a little more about them. Now look back carefully through the story and see if you can spot them all.

Lady Cicily
She is clumsy, and rather accident prone.

Hungry Harry
He is always hungry and eats anything and everything.

Fred Photo
He likes mountain climbing – and photography.

Friendly Flora
She likes to stop and chat with her friends.

Lazy Larry
The fresh mountain air may make this sleepy climber drowsy.

Daredevil Dot
Her daredevil activities can be dangerous.

Fisher Jim
He enjoys climbing, but sometimes he'd rather be fishing.

Katy Climber
She wears baggy trousers, which may trip her up.

Answers

Pages 68-69 Setting off

The other mountain climbers are circled in red.

Pages 70-71 Which path?

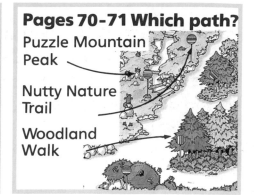

Puzzle Mountain Peak

Nutty Nature Trail

Woodland Walk

Pages 72-73 Mountain musicians

The differences are circled in red.
Can you find the extra differences?

Pages 74-75 Lost goats

The seven missing goats are circled in red.

Pages 76-77 Ice skating

The missing skating partners are circled in red.

Pages 78-79 Food stop

Poppy buys a pastry for two Puzzle Pennies, and a glass of juice for three Puzzle Pennies. For Bernard she buys a tasty bone for two Puzzle Pennies, and a bowl of doggy drink, for three Puzzle Pennies. This adds up to ten Puzzle Pennies exactly.

Pages 80-81 Ski lift

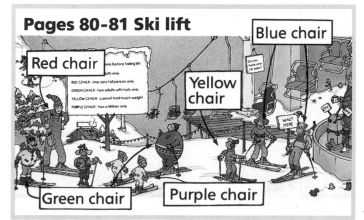

Blue chair

Red chair

Yellow chair

Green chair

Purple chair

Pages 82-83 Sorting the skis

These are Tim's matching skis.

These are his poles.

95

Pages 84-85 Toboggan race

The clear route from the start to the finish of the race is shown in red.

Pages 86-87 Ice walk

The six ice cream cones are circled in red. The safe route across the glacier is shown in black.

Pages 88-89 Nearly there

Poppy has spotted the Yodel flower.

Pages 90-91 Mountain monsters

The super-speedy red toboggan is here.

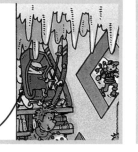

Pages 92-93 Poppy returns

The monster is scaring Basil!

Did you spot everything?

Sports day prizes

The chart below shows you which sports day prize is hidden on which double page.

Pages	Prize
68-69	hiking boot
70-71	little trumpet
72-73	cowbell
74-75	ice skate necklace
76-77	chocolate
78-79	ski jumper on stand
80-81	mini ski pole
82-83	toboggan trophy
84-85	red flag
86-87	snowman pendant
88-89	prize badge
90-91	golden pickaxe

Basil

Puzzle Mountain monster

Basil and the monster

Did you remember to watch out for Basil, and for the Puzzle Mountain monster? Look back through the story and see if you can spot them on each double page.

First published in 1993 by Usborne Publishing Ltd., Usborne House, 83-85 Saffron Hill, London EC1N 8RT, England.

Copyright © 1993 Usborne Publishing Ltd.

The name Usborne and the device 🐝 are Trade Marks of Usborne Publishing Ltd.

Printed in Portugal.